CUTE AND UNUSUAL PETS
MINI PIGS

by Paula Wilson

Consultant
Sarrah Kaye
Veterinarian and General Curator
Staten Island Zoo
Staten Island, New York

CAPSTONE PRESS
a capstone imprint

Snap Books are published by Capstone Press,
1710 Roe Crest Drive, North Mankato, Minnesota 56003
www.mycapstone.com

Copyright © 2019 by Capstone Press, a Capstone imprint. All rights reserved. No part of this publication may be reproduced in whole or in part, or stored in a retrieval system, or transmitted in any form or by any means, electronic, mechanical, photocopying, recording, or otherwise, without written permission of the publisher.

Library of Congress Cataloging-in-Publication Data
Names: Wilson, Paula M., 1963- author.
Title: Mini pigs / by Paula M. Wilson.
Description: North Mankato, Minnesota : an imprint of Capstone Press, [2019]
  | Series: Snap books. Cute and unusual pets. | Audience: Age 8-14.
Identifiers: LCCN 2018016117 (print) | LCCN 2018017758 (ebook) |
  ISBN 9781543530674 (eBook PDF) |
  ISBN 9781543530582 (hardcover)
Subjects: LCSH: Miniature pigs—Juvenile literature.
Classification: LCC SF393.M55 (ebook) | LCC SF393.M55 W55 2019 (print) | DDC
  636.4—dc23
LC record available at https://lccn.loc.gov/2018016117

Editorial Credits
Lauren Dupuis-Perez, editor
Sara Radka, designer
Kathy McColley, production specialist

Image Credits
Getty Images: andresr, 21, 27, balwan, 6, Eriklam, 1, goce, 17, Page Light Studios, 22, SherryL18, 11, Sonsedska, 16; Shutterstock: FoapAB, 29, Goodwyn Ferrell, 5, Jiang Hongyan, back cover, 4, 15, kuban_girl, 19, MikaHolanda, 13, MintImages, cover, Plotitsyna NiNa, 9, TalyaPhoto, 25

Glossary terms are bolded on first use in text.

3 1350 00377 5428

Printed and bound in the United States of America.
PA021

TABLE OF CONTENTS

CHAPTER 1
Meet the Mini Pig................. 4

CHAPTER 2
Pigs as Pets..................... 10

CHAPTER 3
Caring for Your Mini Pig.......... 16

CHAPTER 4
Get to Know Your Mini Pig........ 20

CHAPTER 5
Part of the Community............ 26

Glossary......................... 30
Read More....................... 31
Internet Sites.................... 31
Index............................ 32

CHAPTER 1
MEET THE MINI PIG

If you are looking for a pet that is smart, playful, and clean, a mini pig just might be a good choice. It may surprise you that pigs are clean, but it is true. With some room to roam and dig, mini pigs make great pets.

Pigs, along with chimpanzees and elephants, are some of the smartest **mammals**. Because of this, you can train mini pigs to do all kinds of things. You can teach them to use a litter box, take walks on a leash, and do tricks.

Mini pigs form lifelong bonds with their owners. Many even like to cuddle. Pigs may be nervous when they first come home with you. With proper training and lots of attention, they can quickly become part of the family.

---

mammal—a warm-blooded animal that breathes air; mammals have hair or fur; female mammals feed milk to their young
species—a group of animals with common features

DID YOU KNOW?

Mini pigs belong to one of 16 **species** of pigs. Other species include wild boar, warthogs, and farm pigs.

Mini pigs are about one-tenth the size of a farm pig.

NOT SO MINI

Mini pigs are not as small as you might think. They are little when they are born but do not stay that way. This animal weighs 50 to 150 pounds (23 to 68 kilograms) when fully-grown. It may be 14 to 20 inches (36 to 51 centimeters) tall. Mini pigs are fully grown by 5 years of age. They usually live 15 to 20 years.

A baby pig is called a piglet.

HOW BIG?

Sometimes pet mini pigs grow much larger than their owners expect. The pigs become too big to handle. Unfortunately, some breeders let buyers think that this pet will stay tiny. The owners then take their pigs to animal shelters. More than 50 pig adoption and rescue centers are located in the United States and Canada. These centers have become overcrowded with mini pigs given up for adoption.

A MINI PIG'S BODY

Mini pigs come in a variety of colors. They can be different shades of black, brown, pink, and white. Some are speckled or spotted. Mini pigs look fuzzy, but stiff hair, not fur, covers their bodies. The hair often changes color as they age. Mini pigs have four toes on each foot. The middle toes form a **cloven** hoof. Mini pigs have small ears and a long snout.

DID YOU KNOW?
Pigs have about 15,000 taste buds. Humans only have about 10,000.

---

cloven—a foot that has the front part split into two parts

SNOUTS AND SOUNDS

Mini pigs have a strong sense of smell. They use their snouts to sniff out food. Mini pigs have a natural need to dig. This is called a rooting instinct. Mini pigs root for different reasons. These include looking for food, communicating, or soothing themselves. Pet pigs need a place to root, such as a patch of dirt or a pile of blankets. If they are not allowed to root, they may destroy carpets or gardens.

Mini pigs are social. They like being around people and other pigs. Mini pigs are noisy animals that communicate with grunts, oinks, and squeals. They make these sounds especially when they are hungry, happy, or angry.

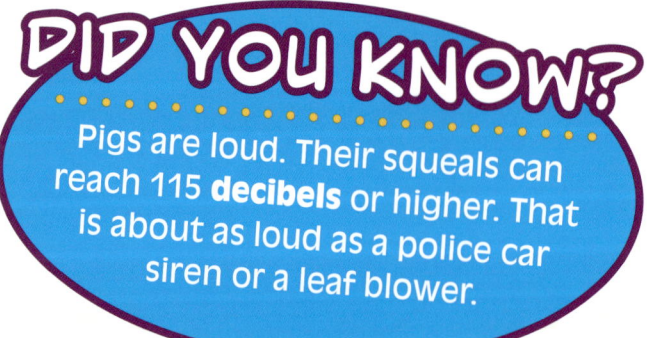

DID YOU KNOW?
Pigs are loud. Their squeals can reach 115 **decibels** or higher. That is about as loud as a police car siren or a leaf blower.

---

decibel—a unit for measuring the volume of sounds

Over time you will get to know what your mini pig's sounds mean.

CHAPTER 2
PIGS AS PETS

Pigs are **descendants** of wild boar. Wild boar are **native** to Asia and Europe. Thousands of years ago, people began to **domesticate** wild boar. Today these animals include farm pigs and pigs kept as pets. Mini pig **breeds** are different from farm pigs. Farm pigs are much larger. They can weigh up to 1,000 pounds (450 kg). They have longer snouts and bigger ears than mini pigs. Mini pigs have shorter legs and narrower bodies than farm pigs.

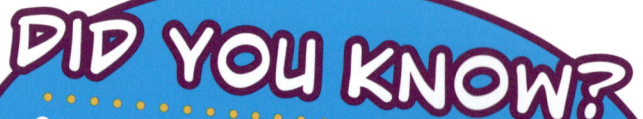

Several celebrities made the pet mini pig a big hit. Singer Miley Cyrus, soccer player David Beckham, and actor George Clooney have all owned pigs. Clooney's pet pig, Max, lived for 18 years.

---

descendant—a person or animal who comes from a particular group of ancestors
native—growing or living naturally in a particular place
domesticate—to tame something so that it can live with or be used by humans
breed—a group of animals that look and act alike

Mini pigs include a variety of pig breeds that have been developed to be smaller in size. This is why mini pigs come in so many different colors.

People began breeding small pigs in the 1960s. The Vietnamese potbelly pig is one of the first small pig breeds. Today's mini pigs are a mix of many different breeds. These include the Vietnamese potbelly, the Kunekune pig from New Zealand, and the Göttingen pig from Europe. Mini pigs first arrived in the United States in the 1980s, mainly for use in zoos. There, people fell in love with them and wanted them as pets. The mini pig trend caught on. Mini pigs are now popular pets in North America, South America, and Europe.

IS A MINI PIG RIGHT FOR YOU?

Caring for a pet is a big responsibility, especially a pet that can grow to the size of a large dog. Mini pigs need daily attention. Talk to your parents about owning a pet pig. Answer these questions to help decide if a mini pig is right for you and your family:

- Do you have the time to care for a mini pig, including feeding, cleaning, and playing with it?

- Who will take care of the mini pig, feeding it every day and cleaning up after it? You or your parents or siblings? Or will you all share in the responsibility?

- How much does a mini pig cost to buy and feed? Who will take on the financial responsibility? You or your parents?

- Do you have space in your home and in your yard for a mini pig? Do you have an area for it to root?

- Is it legal to have a pet mini pig in your town or city?

- Do the vets in your area take care of mini pigs?

NOT ALWAYS WELCOME

Some cities and towns do not allow pigs to be kept as pets. These communities consider all pigs to be farm animals and require them to live on a farm. Laws are different from town to town. Pet pigs, big or little, are not allowed in New York City, Chicago, or Boston. However, they are allowed in cities such as Seattle, Las Vegas, and Kansas City. Make sure mini pigs are allowed as pets where you live before adopting one.

Mini pigs can be a lot of work. They need attention every day.

PIG PLACES

You've decided a mini pig is right for you. Where do you get one? A breeder can help you choose a pet and show you how to take care of it. Go to a breeder who is registered with the American Mini Pig Association. Another option is to find an an animal shelter in your area that has mini pigs to adopt.

Find a breeder who spends a lot of time interacting with, or socializing, their pigs. A socialized pig can usually **adapt** easily to you and your home. The best time to take a mini pig home is when it is between 6 and 8 weeks old. Check with the breeder or adoption agency to make sure your mini pig is **neutered** or **spayed**.

DID YOU KNOW?
Mini pigs can cost anywhere from $500 to more than $1,000.

---

adapt—to change to fit into a new or different environment
neuter—to operate on a male animal so it is unable to produce young
spay—to operate on a female animal so it is unable to produce young

Choosing a mini pig that is healthy is important. Look for a pig that is friendly and not afraid of people. Another sign of good health is clear and bright eyes. Also, a pig's skin should be smooth with no rashes or bumps. Some people buy more than one mini pig. They are social animals that like to be with other pigs. However, most pig owners do not have the proper amount of space for two or more mini pigs.

PIG EXPERTS

The American Mini Pig Association educates owners, breeders, and the public about mini pigs. The association promotes healthy breeding practices. With newsletters, webinars, and a website, the association encourages the proper care of mini pigs. Owners use the association as a resource for all sorts of mini pig information, such as how to keep mini pigs healthy. The association also provides tips for training mini pigs.

CHAPTER 3
CARING FOR YOUR MINI PIG

Mini pigs need plenty of room, both indoors and outdoors. Find a spot in your house that your pet can call its own. A penned-in area with blankets and pillows works well. Your pig will need a litter box that is easy to get to and that is set apart from its bedding area. It will also need a sturdy water bowl filled with fresh, clean water for it to drink.

Outside your mini pig will need room for running, grazing, and exploring. Be sure to keep your pig fenced in so that it does not get loose. It also needs an area where it can root in the dirt.

Pigs do not sweat very much. Mud helps cool them down.

WATCH THE WEATHER

During warmer months be sure your mini pig does not get overheated. Rolling in water or mud helps cool it off on a hot day. A kiddie pool filled with water also helps to cool a pig. Your mini pig should have a shady area to get away from the hot sun. Pigs can get sunburned just like humans. Put sunscreen on your pig to help protect its skin. Rolling around in the mud also prevents sunburn. The mud coating acts as a sunscreen.

Be sure to keep your pig warm during winter months. Help your mini pig adjust to colder weather. Bring it outside for short periods of time. Do not leave your pig outside for long when it is extremely cold.

PIG FOOD

Mini pigs need a well-balanced diet. Feed them pellets made for mini pigs. Do not feed them pellets for farm pigs. Mini pigs also need fresh vegetables, such as squash and leafy greens. Fatty and salty foods should be avoided. Do not underfeed your mini pig to keep it small. Overfeeding is also a problem because pigs can quickly become overweight. If they are not fed properly, mini pigs can have serious health and behavior issues. According to the American Mini Pig Association, mini pigs should eat about 2 percent of their ideal weight each day.

A VET FOR YOUR PET

Find a veterinarian in your area who is familiar with mini pigs. Pet pigs should visit the vet regularly for **vaccinations**. Your veterinarian will also test your pig for **parasites** and give it medicine if needed.

---

vaccination—a shot of medicine that protects from a disease
parasite—an animal or plant that lives on other animals or plants

A PAMPERED PIG

Mini pigs need their hooves trimmed, especially if they do not dig in dirt regularly. You or your vet can trim your pet's hooves. If you trim them yourself, be very careful not to trim too deeply. This can be painful to your pig.

You do not need to bathe your pig often unless it is covered in dirt or mud. The best way to bathe it is in the bathtub with warm water. It may not like bath time. Your pig will let you know this with its loud squeals. Let it get used to the water. Put small treats in the tub to help calm your pig. Use a soft cloth to clean its eyes and ears. Mini pigs often have dry skin so be sure not to bathe your pig too often.

DID YOU KNOW?

Mini pigs shed their hair, called "blowing their coat," once or twice a year. New hair starts to grow in soon after the old hair is gone.

CHAPTER 4
GET TO KNOW YOUR MINI PIG

Gaining your mini pig's trust will take time. When you first bring your pig home, give it time to adjust to its new surroundings. Start slowly. First spend time sitting on the floor next to your pig. Give it small treats to show that you are not a threat. Talk to your pig to help it get used to your voice. Grabbing or picking up a mini pig can cause it anxiety until it trusts you. Mini pigs feel threatened if their feet are not on the ground. Eventually your pig will get closer to you. It may even sit in your lap. Other members of your family should also spend time with the pet.

Do you have other pets at home? If so, introduce them to your pig slowly so they become comfortable with each other. Some breeders recommend never leaving a dog alone with a mini pig. Dogs may harm mini pigs.

DID YOU KNOW?
Pigs are hypoallergenic. People who are allergic to some pets, such as dogs and cats, are not allergic to mini pigs.

Spending time with your pig is the best way to form a lasting bond.

What happens if you brought a mini pig home, but then realize it is not the right pet for your family? Do not let the pig free. Pet pigs do not have the skills to survive in the wild. Find a home for the mini pig with a breeder or with someone who wants to adopt it.

Many mini pig owners enjoy teaching their pets to do fun tricks.

WHO'S THE BOSS?

Begin setting boundaries once your pig feels comfortable with you. Your pig may think that it is the **dominant** one in the family. You want your pig to know that you are the boss. Do not let your mini pig move into your personal space whenever it wants. Once you've trained your pig, make sure it obeys your commands to sit or stay. Use a firm voice, but do not yell at your pig. Consistently enforce your rules. Keep a strict routine. This helps your pig know that you are in charge.

Mini pigs are usually easy to train, especially when treats are involved. Start training your pig when it is very young. Using a litter box is one of the most important things for it to learn. You can also train your pig to sit, stay, shake hands, and turn in circles. More advanced tricks include walking in a figure eight pattern and waving. The American Mini Pig Association website has tips for training this pet.

---

dominant—very powerful or important

A PLEASED PIG

Mini pigs can get bored easily. They need activities to keep them busy. A bored pig can become destructive and aggressive. Keeping your pig active is also good for its health. Make sure your pet has plenty of time to dig and roam outside. Interact with your pet often. Pigs love to have their bellies rubbed and their skin brushed.

You can play all sorts of fun and enriching games with your mini pig. Mini pigs especially love games that involve food. Some pig owners make a food ball for their pet. Buy a plastic ball with holes from a pet store and put snacks inside. Your pig will spend lots of time trying to get the food out of the ball. Try hiding snacks in a hay pile or in the yard. This gives your pig the chance to root around for the treats. If you have some old newspapers or magazines, give them to your mini pig. It will enjoy shredding the paper.

DID YOU KNOW?
Anne Langton holds the Guinness World Record for the largest collection of pig-related items—16,779 to be exact. Her collection includes piggy banks, stuffed toys, and glass figurines all shaped like pigs.

Giving your pig items to play with outside will keep your pet active and happy.

Another great way to keep your pig active is to set up an obstacle course in your yard. Your mini pig will quickly figure out how to move through the course. You can also run around the yard together or take your pig for a walk on a leash.

CHAPTER 5
PART OF THE COMMUNITY

Mini pigs are comfortable around people. They can even lend a helping hand—or hoof. Therapy pets visit people in the community. They provide comfort, enjoyment, and help with disabilities. Mini pigs make great therapy pets. Different animal organizations, including the American Mini Pig Association, can certify pigs as therapy pets. To become certified, pigs need to obey certain commands. They should be comfortable in crowds and not mind being touched. Therapy pigs should also be friendly and have an easygoing manner.

Some pig owners bring their pigs to visit schools and libraries. There, pig owners educate people about mini pigs. Other pigs visit nursing homes and hospitals. These pigs help ease anxiety. They comfort people who do not feel well.

DID YOU KNOW?
A mini pig named Hank has become an Internet sensation. He has more than 347,000 Instagram followers. Hank has even made an appearance at a Sacramento Kings basketball game!

Most mini pigs like being around humans and other pigs.

PART OF THE FAMILY

Each mini pig has a unique personality. From a young age, a mini pig bonds with its owners and becomes a member of the family. Compared to most pets, mini pigs live long lives. Your mini pig could be a part of your family for 20 years. Mini pigs are wonderful pets, but they are a lot of work. Before getting a pet pig, make sure you have the right amount of space and enough time to care for it. If you take the time to bond with your pig and keep it healthy, you can enjoy the companionship of your pig for many years.

NERVOUS FLYER? PET A DOG . . . OR A PIG
The San Francisco International Airport has a program called the Wag Brigade. Airplane travel can be stressful. Because of this, the airport brings in trained dogs to cheer up travelers and calm their nerves. A mini pig named LiLou is the first pig to join the Wag Brigade. LiLou performs fun tricks to entertain travelers. All the animals in the Wag Brigade wear vests that say "Pet Me!"

Many pigs are happiest when included in family life.

Learn all that you can about mini pigs both before and after adopting one. Read books and have an adult help you research mini pigs online. Consider joining a mini pig club to get to know other mini pig owners. The more you know about these adorable pets, the better you can care for one.

GLOSSARY

adapt (uh-DAPT)—to change to fit into a new or different environment

breed (BREED)—a group of animals that look and act alike

cloven (KLOH-vin)—a foot that has the front part split into two parts

decibel (DE-suh-buhl)—a unit for measuring the volume of sounds

descendant (dih-SEN-dent)—a person or animal who comes from a particular group of ancestors

domesticate (duh-MESS-tuh-kate)—to tame something so that it can live with or be used by humans

dominant (DOM-uh-nuh-nt)—very powerful or important

mammal (MAM-uhl)—a warm–blooded animal that breathes air; mammals have hair or fur; female mammals feed milk to their young

native (NAY-tiv)—growing or living naturally in a particular place

neuter (NOO-tur)—to operate on a male animal so it is unable to produce young

parasite (PEH-ruh-sait)—an animal or plant that lives on other animals or plants

spay (SPAY)—to operate on a female animal so it is unable to produce young

species (SPEE-sheez)—a group of animals with common features

vaccination (vak-sih-NAY-shun)—a shot of medicine that protects from a disease

READ MORE

Boothroyd, Jennifer. *Meet a Baby Pig*. Baby Farm Animals. Minneapolis: Lerner Publications, 2017.

Reed, Cristie. *Mini Pig*. You Have a Pet What?! Vero Beach, Fla.: Rourke Educational Media, 2015.

Silverman, Buffy. *Mini Pigs*. Little Pets. Minneapolis: Lerner Publications, 2018.

Tasker, Pamela. *Potbellied Pigs*. Our Weird Pets. New York: PowerKids Press, 2018.

Thatcher, Henry. *Wild Boars and Teacup Pigs*. Big Animals, Small Animals. New York: PowerKids Press, 2014.

INTERNET SITES

Use FactHound to find Internet sites related to this book.

Visit *www.facthound.com*

Just type in 9781543530582 and go.

Check out projects, games and lots more at
www.capstonekids.com

INDEX

American Mini Pig Association, 14, 15, 18, 23, 26

bathing, 19
breeders, 7, 14, 15, 20, 21

cleaning, 12
colors, 7
cost, 12, 14

feeding, 4, 8, 12, 18, 19, 20, 23, 24

hooves, 19

laws, 12, 13
life span, 6, 28
litter boxes, 4, 16, 23

playing, 12, 24

rooting, 8, 12, 16, 24

size, 6, 7, 12
sounds, 8, 19
sunburn, 17

therapy pets, 26
training, 4, 15, 23, 28

veterinarians, 12, 18, 19